The Butter Thief

Story by Chris Murray
Illustrated by Kim Waters Murray

For Our Son,
David

Mandala Publishing Group
103 Thomason Lane
Eugene, OR 97404
phone: 800 688 2218
fax: 541 461 3478
mandala@mandala.org

1585-A Folsom Street
San Francisco, CA 94103
phone: 415 626 1080
fax: 415 626 1510

239C Joo Chiat Road
Singapore 427496
phone: 65 342 3117
fax: 65 342 3115

Adapted from the writings of
His Divine Grace A.C. Bhaktivedanta Swami Prabhupada

Printed in Hong Kong through Palace Press International

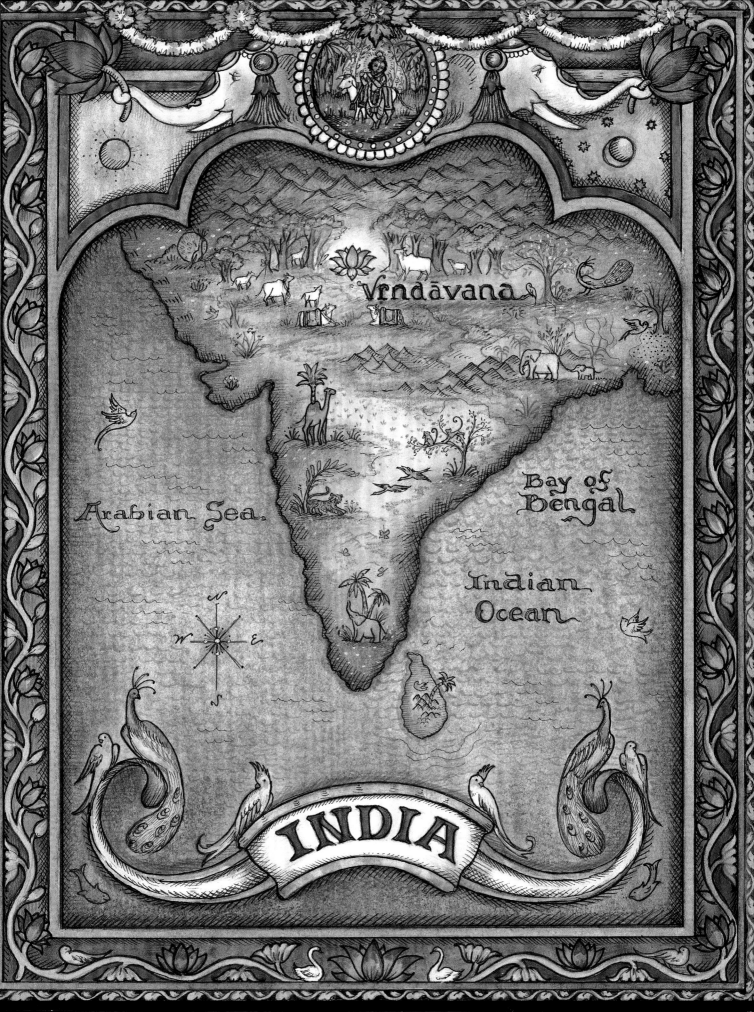

Long ago in India there lived the most wonderful child. His name was Krishna, and he lived very happily with his mother and father in the beautiful village of Vrindavana.

In Vrindavana the homes were very pleasant. The forests were full of beautiful birds and peacocks. The rivers flowed with pure water, and the pasturing grounds were full of cows. All around there were signs of good fortune.

One day, Mother Yasoda was churning butter. As she worked, she made up songs about her little Krishna. She looked very beautiful as she pulled on the churning rope.

While she was busy working, Krishna came to her and wanted to be fed.

Mother Yasoda loved Krishna very much and was always happy to take care of him. She stopped her work and hugged her darling Krishna. She let him sit on her lap and looked at his face with great affection.

While Mother Yasoda was nursing Krishna, she suddenly remembered the pan of milk she had left to boil on the stove. Quickly Yasoda left Krishna to take care of the over-flowing milk.

When Yasoda left, Krishna became very angry, and he broke the pot of freshly churned butter. Quickly he ran to another room to eat it.

After Yasoda took care of the overflowing milk, she turned and saw what naughty Krishna had done.

She followed his butter-smeared footprints right into the storage room.

There was Krishna sitting on a big wooden mortar, giving butter and yogurt to the monkeys.

Krishna suddenly heard his mother coming and quickly got down and ran away. Yasoda chased after him, and finally captured him.

Mother Yasoda took Krishna by the hand and told him he had been a naughty boy.

To keep Krishna from getting into more trouble, Mother Yasoda tied him by his waist to the wooden mortar.

When Yasoda was busy back at work, Krishna saw two trees standing side by side. He began to crawl toward the trees, pulling the wooden mortar behind him. As he passed between the trees, the large mortar became stuck. Krishna pulled very hard on the rope, and the two trees came crashing down with a great sound.

Out of the trees appeared two beautiful men, shining like the sun. They had been cursed long ago to become trees, but now they had been freed by Krishna. They bowed before him again and again, thanking him, and then they left.

After hearing the sounds of the crashing trees, everyone rushed to the spot and looked in amazement.

The children who had been playing nearby told how Krishna had pulled down the two trees, and how two wonderful-looking men had appeared and spoken with him.

Krishna's father Nanda Maharaja smiled upon hearing about his son. He untied the rope around Krishna's waist and set him free.

In the courtyard of his house the women and children gathered and began to clap and sing while Krishna danced for them.

Simply by loving Krishna, everyone became happy.